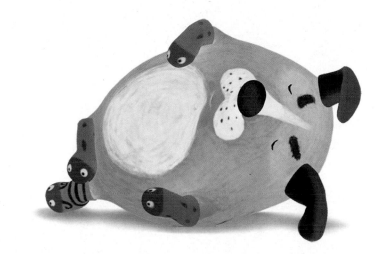

THE BRAZIER AND HIS DOG

Why should we do our part to help others?

www.av2books.com

Go to **www.av2books.com**, and enter this book's unique code.

BOOK CODE

Y69680

AV² by Weigl brings you media enhanced books that support active learning.

Published by AV² by Weigl
350 5th Avenue, 59th Floor New York, NY 10118
Websites: www.av2books.com   www.weigl.com

Library of Congress Cataloging-in-Publication Data

The brazier and his dog / Aesop.
    pages cm. -- (Storytime)
 Summary: "In The Brazier and His Dog, Aesop and his troupe teach their audience the value of doing our share of a job. They learn that we shouldn't expect others to do our part"-- Provided by publisher.
 ISBN 978-1-4896-2449-9 (hardcover : alk. paper) -- ISBN 978-1-4896-2450-5 (single user ebook) -- ISBN 978-1-4896-2451-2 (multi user ebook)
[1. Fables. 2. Folklore.] I. Aesop.
 PZ8.2.B6673 2014
 398.2--dc23
 [E]
                                    2014009681

Printed in the United States in North Mankato, Minnesota
1 2 3 4 5 6 7 8 9 0 18 17 16 15 14

052014
WEP090514

FABLE SYNOPSIS

For thousands of years, parents and teachers have used memorable stories called fables to teach simple moral lessons to children.

In the Aesop's Fables by AV² series, classic fables are given a lighthearted twist. These familiar tales are performed by a troupe of animal players whose endearing personalities bring the stories to life.

In *The Brazier and His Dog*, Aesop and his troupe teach their audience the value of doing their share of a job. They learn that they should not expect others to do their part.

This AV² media enhanced book comes alive with...

Animated Video
Watch a custom animated movie.

Try This!
Complete activities and hands-on experiments.

Key Words
Study vocabulary, and complete a matching word activity.

Quiz
Test your knowledge.

THE BRAZIER AND HIS DOG

Why should we do our part to help others?

AV² Storytime Navigation

TRY THIS

KEY WORDS

Quiz

PLAY/PAUSE MOVIE

CLOSE

HOME

VIDEO LENGTH

VOLUME

INFO

TITLE INFORMATION

STORYTIME

The Players

Aesop
I am the leader of Aesop's Theater, a screenwriter, and an actor.
I can be hot-tempered, but I am also soft and warm-hearted.

Libbit
I am an actor and a prop man.
I think I should have been a lion, but I was born a rabbit.

Presy
I am the manager of Aesop's Theater.
I am also the narrator of the plays.

Elvis
I like dance and music. I am artistic. I am very good at drawing.

Bogart
I am the strongest and the oldest pig. I always do whatever I want.

Audrey
I am a very good and caring pig. If someone cries, I cry with them. I never lie.

Milala
I think I am cute. I like to get attention from the other animals.

Goddard
I am very greedy. I like food.

The Story

One afternoon, Goddard was lying on a sofa.

He felt like having a lazy day.

"It's a nice day today.

Let's clean up!" said Presy.

Goddard yawned and

pretended to fall asleep.

Presy started giving directions to the Shorties.

"Bogart, clean the carriage. Audrey, clean the bottles.

Elvis and Milala, clean the stage. Goddard...

Wait, where's Goddard?"

"I don't see him!" said Libbit.

Presy looked around.

She saw Goddard sleeping on the sofa.

Bogart, Audrey, Elvis, and Milala started to clean.

Bogart knocked a plant pot to the ground.

Elvis and Milala came to clean up the mess.

Audrey was in a corner cleaning bottles.

Goddard was still sleeping on the sofa.

The Shorties had finished cleaning.

"You all deserve a snack for your hard work," said Presy.

Presy handed out cheese and lemonade.

The four Shorties ate and drank happily.

13

Goddard heard them eating and walked up to the table.

He took Bogart's cheese and ate it.

Bogart got very angry.

"You didn't help us! We earned this food!" said Bogart.

Goddard didn't care. He also drank Elvis' lemonade.

"Goddard has given me an idea for a new play," said Aesop.

"I think it will teach him a lesson," continued Aesop.

"The new play is called *The Brazier and His Dog*."

There once was a hard-working brazier.

The brazier worked all day long while his dog slept.

The brazier struck his hammer loudly,

but his dog did not wake up.

The noise was so loud that the brazier wondered...

Was his dog only pretending to sleep?

The brazier took a break for lunch.

When he started to eat, his dog awoke.

The dog barked for food.

"You only woke up because I was eating," said the brazier.

"Why do you deserve food when you haven't done any work?"

The brazier kicked the dog out of his house.

After the play, Goddard went to lie down on the sofa.

"Everyone, let's clean the stage," said Presy.

Goddard heard Presy, but he pretended to sleep.

He was feeling too lazy to help out.

Presy had played a trick on Goddard.

Instead of cleaning, Presy was giving food to everyone.

"Keep scrubbing the floor, Elvis," said Presy as she handed him a square of cheese.

"Polish those bottles, Audrey," said Presy.

Aesop chuckled as Presy handed him some cheese.

While they ate, Goddard still pretended to sleep.

When lunch was finished, the Shorties began to clean up.

Goddard heard the plates being stacked.

He rushed to the table.

"Where's my food?" asked Goddard.

"You only woke up for food," said Presy. "But when
you thought we were working, you pretended to sleep."

Goddard sat down in front of a plate and sighed.

Only one small pea was left.

If you want to share in the reward,

do not expect others to do your part.

What is a Story?

Players

Who is the story about? The characters, or players, are the people, animals, or objects that perform the story. Characters have personality traits that contribute to the story. Readers understand how a character fits into the story by what the character says and does, what others say about the character, and how others treat the character.

Setting

Where and when do the events take place? The setting of a story helps readers visualize where and when the story is taking place. These details help to suggest the mood or atmosphere of the story. A setting is usually presented briefly, but it explains whether the story is taking place in the past, present, or future and in a large or small area.

Plot

What happens in the story? The plot is a story's plan of action. Most plots follow a pattern. They begin with an introduction and progress to the rising action of events. The events lead to a climax, which is the most exciting moment in the story. The resolution is the falling action of events. This section ties up loose ends so that readers are not left with unanswered questions. The story ends with a conclusion that brings the events to a close.

Point of View

Who is telling the story? The story is normally told from the point of view of the narrator, or storyteller. The narrator can be a main character or a less important character in the story. He or she can also be someone who is not in the story but is observing the action. This observer may be impartial or someone who knows the thoughts and feelings of the characters. A story can also be told from different points of view.

Dialogue

What type of conversation occurs in the story? Conversation, or dialogue, helps to show what is happening. It also gives information about the characters. The reader can discover what kinds of people they are by the words they say and how they say them. Writers use dialogue to make stories more interesting. In dialogue, writers imitate the way real people speak, so it is written differently than the rest of the story.

Theme

What is the story's underlying meaning? The theme of a story is the topic, idea, or position that the story presents. It is often a general statement about life. Sometimes, the theme is stated clearly. Other times, it is suggested through hints.

THE BRAZIER AND HIS DOG Quiz

1 Who was sleeping on the sofa?

2 Who knocked over the plant pot?

3 What did Goddard take from Bogart?

4 What did Goddard take from Elvis?

5 What tool did the brazier use?

6 Why did the brazier kick his dog out of the house?

Key Words

Research has shown that as much as 65 percent of all written material published in English is made up of 300 words. These 300 words cannot be taught using pictures or learned by sounding them out. They must be recognized by sight. This book contains 104 common sight words to help young readers improve their reading fluency and comprehension. This book also teaches young readers several important content words, such as proper nouns. These words are paired with pictures to aid in learning and improve understanding.

Page	Sight Words First Appearance
4	a, also, am, an, and, be, been, but, can, have, I, of, plays, should, the, think, was
5	always, animals, at, do, food, from, get, good, if, like, never, other, them, to, very, want, with
6	day, he, it's, on, one, said, up
8	around, don't, him, saw, see, she, started
11	came, in, still
12	all, for, four, had, hard, out, work, you, your
15	got, help, it, this, took, us, walked, we
16	has, idea, me, new, will
18	did, long, not, once, only, so, there, while
21	any, because, eat, house, when, why
23	after, down, too, went
25	as, keep, some, those
27	asked, began, being, left, my, part, small, though, were

Page	Content Words First Appearance
4	actor, leader, lion, manager, narrator, prop man, rabbit, screenwriter, theater
5	dance, music, pig
6	afternoon, sofa
8	bottles, carriage, stage
11	ground, plant pot
12	cheese, lemonade, snack
15	table
16	brazier, dog
18	hammer, noise
21	lunch
25	floor
27	pea, plates

Check out av2books.com for your animated storytime media enhanced book!

1 Go to av2books.com

2 Enter book code   Y69680

3 Fuel your imagination online!

www.av2books.com

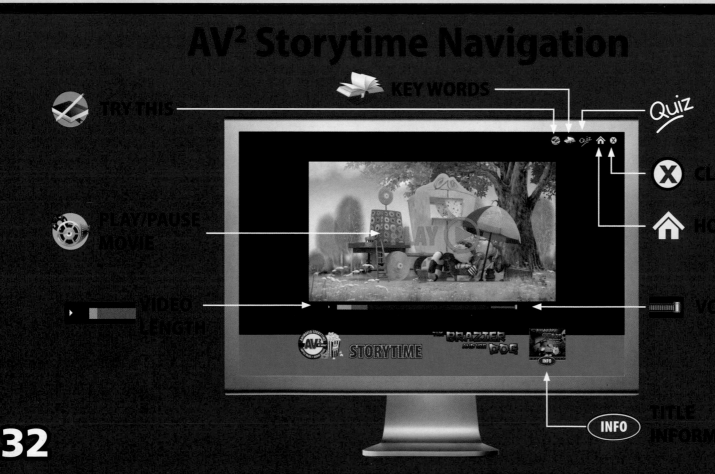

AV² Storytime Navigation

KEY WORDS

TRY THIS

Quiz

CLOSE

PLAY/PAUSE MOVIE

HOME

VIDEO LENGTH

VOLUME

STORYTIME

INFO

INFO

TITLE INFORMATION